DETEKTIV

Wolfgang Ecke

The House of the 99 Ghosts

Wolfgang Ecke

Sein Name ist zu einem Begriff für gute, spannende Unterhaltung geworden. Spannung nicht durch sensationelle Gewalt, sondern aus der Aufforderung zum Mitdenken und durch lebendige Dialoge.
Er hat über 600 Hörspiele geschrieben, von denen unzählige, ebenso wie ein Großteil seiner Bücher in viele Sprachen übersetzt wurden. Er war ständiger Mitarbeiter bei Radiosendern im In- und Ausland, schrieb für Jugendzeitschriften und produzierte Platten und Fernsehfilme.

Von Wolfgang Ecke sind in den Ravensburger Taschenbüchern außerdem erschienen:

RTB 1603
Geister, Spuk und Nachtgespenster

RTB 2037
The Face at the Window

RTB 2063
Der Mann in Schwarz

RTB 2065
Das Haus der 99 Geister

RTB 2068
The Man in Black

RTB 2076
Club der Detektive

RTB 2096
Gauner, Gangster, Geistesblitze

The House of the 99 Ghosts

and other
detective stories

RAVENSBURGER BUCHVERLAG

Illustrations by Stephan Kaluza

Als Ravensburger Taschenbuch
Band 2081
erschienen 1997
Erstmals in den Ravensburger
Taschenbüchern erschienen 1981
(als RTB 718)

Die Geschichten erschienen 1972,
1973, 1974 als deutsche Originalausgaben
in folgenden Ravensburger Taschenbüchern:
RTB 227 Solo für Melodica
RTB 264 Das Geheimnis der alten Dschunke
RTB 306 Das Haus der 99 Geister

Die englische Erstausgabe erschien 1979
bei Methuen Children's Books Ltd., London
unter dem Titel "Be A Super Sleuth
with the Case of the Stolen Paintings"

Aus dem Deutschen
von Stella und Vernon Humphries
Bearbeitung: Uwe Lüer

Umschlagillustration: Stephan Kaluza

RTB-Reihenkonzeption:
Heinrich Paravicini, Jens Schmidt

**Gesamtherstellung: Clausen & Bosse, Leck
Printed in Germany**

**Die Rechtschreibung des deutsch-
sprachigen Textes entspricht den Regeln
der neuen Rechtschreibung.**

6 5 4 3 2 1 02 01 00 99 98 97

ISBN 3-473-52081-0

DETEKTIV

CONTENTS

CONTENTS

Solutions:

☆ easy

☆☆ quite difficult

☆☆☆ difficult

Hinweis *Schwierige Vokabeln werden nur beim ersten Auftreten in den Fußnoten unten auf der Seite aufgeführt, ansonsten im alphabetischen Gesamtverzeichnis. Andere Vokabeln sind nur im alphabetischen Gesamtverzeichnis am Schluss des Buches zu finden. Es empfiehlt sich also, häufiger dort nachzuschlagen.*

The left-luggage locker thieves 1

The number of thefts from left-luggage lockers suddenly increased at the railway stations of six large towns in southern Germany.

These thefts never happened at the same time in the six towns, which suggested that they were the work of a gang travelling from town to town. The system was simple, and that's why it was so successful.

There were no broken locks nor any other traces of force. The method was as follows. They hired several lockers in the ordinary way: put in money and took the keys. Then they made duplicate keys and replaced the originals in the locker doors. They then waited until the lockers to which they possessed the new keys were used by unsuspecting travellers.

But these locker thieves made one serious error, so giving the crime squad the opportunity of setting a trap for them. The error they made was that, after some time, they started following a routine, and always visited the stations in the

left-luggage locker	– Gepäckschließfach
theft	– Diebstahl
to increase	– zunehmen
to suggest	– vermuten (lassen)
gang	– Bande
lock	– Schloss
trace	– Spur
force	– Gewalt
unsuspecting	– ahnungslos
crime squad	– Einheit zur Bekämpfung von Verbrechen
to set a trap	– eine Falle stellen

same sequence. This was: **Frankfurt – Stuttgart – Ulm – Munich – Nuremberg – Würzburg – Frankfurt – Stuttgart – Ulm**, and so on. According to the police calculations, therefore, the next station must be Munich and that by the beginning of October. From 4 October onwards, a round-the-clock vigil was arranged. Four officers were stationed not far from the lockers, and all four had been picked for their excellent memories.

By the evening of 5 October, the pattern of crime was already repeating itself. A lady reported the loss of two suitcases with valuable contents. Fifteen hours later, all the photographic equipment of a newspaper photographer disappeared from locker 128.

On Wednesday 7 October, the trap closed. One of the policemen remembered the face of a man he had definitely seen several times lurking near the lockers during the last few days.

This suspect went to locker 52 and from it he took a case which seemed to be rather heavy.

Even before he could leave the station, the detective was at his elbow, steering him towards the office of the railway police.

sequence	– (Reihen-)Folge
vigil	– Wache
pattern	– Muster, Modell; Plan
contents	– Inhalt
equipment	– Ausrüstung
to lurk	– lauern, (herum-)schleichen
suspect	– Verdächtiger
to steer	– steuern, führen

" On Wednesday 7 October,
The trap closed ... "

The man pretended to be most surprised and annoyed, and protested his innocence. He didn't hesitate when he was asked to tell what was inside the case. And his list turned out to be completely correct when the case was opened. The fact that in spite of this he was arrested, and that he really turned out to be one of the thieves, was due only to the discovery of one item which came to light when his pockets were searched.

What was the item?

to pretend	– vorgeben, vortäuschen
to protest	– hier: beteuern
innocence	– Unschuld
to hesitate	– zögern
to be due to	– zurückzuführen sein auf
item	– Beweisstück

The film show 2

Mr Bremer had spent an hour queuing for tickets for the special children's film show. The name of the film, a thriller, was *The Night Owl*. The performance for which he wanted tickets was that of the following day, a Saturday.
However, instead of the four tickets Mr Bremer had asked for, he had got only three, a fact that upset him. Which of his four sons would have to stay at home?
You can imagine how unhappy he felt when he came home. "Listen, boys," he began. "I managed to get tickets for tomorrow's performance, but ..." His words were drowned in cheers from John, Peter, Chris, and Mike. And it was several minutes before he could continue. "Unfortunately, they wouldn't let me have more than three tickets, so one of you will have to stay at home. Who'll volunteer?"
Silence. All four boys suddenly started to stare at the carpet.
"No one, I take it," said Mr Bremer, hardly surprised.
John, the eldest, who was fourteen, raised his head. "We could toss for it, Dad," he said.
"Tossing up is a rotten way," grunted Mike, pulling a face.

to queue	– Schlange stehen
owl	– Eule
performance	– Vorstellung
to upset	– hier: in Verlegenheit bringen
to volunteer	– sich freiwillig melden
to toss	– (Münze) werfen
rotten way	– hier: blöder Vorschlag

He must have had unfortunate experiences with tossing up in the past.

"I know something!" Mr Bremer suddenly said. "Wait here a moment. I'll be back in a minute," he said as he hurried out.

The boys heard him ringing a neighbour's door-bell, and three minutes later he was back, waving a magazine. "I've just borrowed this from next door," he announced.

"But we've plenty of magazines here," said Chris, surprised.

"Not this particular one. There's a special story in it called The Detective Club, and it contains several mistakes. I want you all to read this by yourselves, and the three of you who come closest to finding the right number of mistakes will be the ones who go to the film show. All agreed?" The four boys nodded.

John began, and this is what he read:

Arnold Weingold, a rich crook, lived in Zurich where he was esteemed and admired by the underworld. He didn't bother with petty crime. When he started something, there had to be big money in it. He told two of his cronies to come to see him on 14 September, which was

unfortunate	– unglücklich
this particular one	– genau diese
crook	– Gauner
to esteem	– (hoch) schätzen
to bother with	– sich abgeben mit
petty crime	– unbedeutende Verbrechen, „kleine Fische“
crony	– Kumpel

TICKET
TICKET
TICKET
... who go to the films free. All agreed?

a Thursday, at his beautiful one-room flat, for which he paid a rent of 800 Marks. From there he had a wonderful view over Lake Lucerne. His living-room, dining-room, and bedroom were all furnished with costly antiques. The men arrived punctually and Weingold explained his plan. "On Sunday, I'm going to pay a visit to a private gambling club in Winterthur. Everything is arranged. I think it'll bring us at least seven to eight-hundred thousand in cash, all in all."

Kurt, Sandy and Matt listened carefully to Weingold's words. And in the end they agreed that the plan was very well worked out and provided for all eventualities.

gambling club – (Glücks-)Spiel-Club
to provide for – Vorkehrungen treffen

On 18 September towards 8 p.m. they set out from Zurich. It was a normal Sunday evening, no different from any other. Forty-five minutes later they arrived at the innocent-looking house in Zurich Street, Winterthur. Anyone who didn't know that the gambling club was there must have wondered who owned all the large expensive cars parked outside.

Everything went according to plan. Before the seventy or so visitors to the club realized what was happening Arnold Weingold and his gang were already on their way out. And yet the adventure failed.

Weingold couldn't have guessed that a Zurich detective named Klosterberg, who knew the villain well by sight, was sitting in one of those parked cars and had been keeping a watch on the house for several hours. Actually, he was after a fellow known as Stucki, who was suspected of passing forged currency and who was expected to turn up at the club that same evening. Klosterberg at once knew what the appearance of Weingold and his friends meant, and he immediately raised the alarm over his radio. When the robbers reached their car, they received a nasty shock. Fourteen policemen, after all, are anything but a pleasant surprise – at least for crooks!"

according to	– entsprechend
to fail	– danebengehen
villain	– Schurke
forged currency	– gefälschtes Geld

When John had finished reading he passed the magazine to Peter and whispered "Five!" in his father's ear. Peter thought there were four mistakes, Chris believed there were six, and Mike said he had found seven.

Now it's up to you to decide which of the four boys had to stay at home.

Opportunity makes a thief 3

It was a clear starry night. Almost everyone in the city was fast asleep. Only night-watchmen, late party-goers, and hotel porters were still up and about. And, of course, those for whom darkness is their best friend. Henry Newman, for instance, the notorious thief, whose speciality was breaking into department stores.

He was out on a job tonight.

He'd found a way into the car park of the Great Central Store and from there had no trouble getting into the store itself. Henry Newman certainly was no beginner! He knew the store inside out, and he knew exactly which goods could be sold most profitably later.

After little more than an hour the two cases he had brought with him were stuffed with the articles he had selected: eight of the best cameras on the market, two cassette recorders, twelve diamond rings from the jewellery department, as well as twenty-four gold bracelets, four pearl necklaces, and

opportunity makes a thief	– Gelegenheit macht Diebe
starry	– voller Sterne
notorious	– bekannt, berüchtigt
department store	– Warenhaus
... inside out	– ... wie seine Westentasche
profitable	– Gewinn bringend
department	– Abteilung
bracelet	– Armband
necklace	– Halsband

six diamond-studded tiepins. In the watch department he helped himself to nineteen men's and twenty-six ladies' gold watches, the most expensive ones, of course. And finally he also stole three pairs of binoculars, a microscope and three silver cigarette-cases.

Newman carefully rearranged the displays in the various showcases he had rifled, so that the night-watchman on his patrols would not notice that something was wrong.

It was only later that the bomb went off – when the sales staff arrived that morning at their usual time and discovered the thefts.

At 8.15 a.m., the excited manager rang the police, and he also gave instructions to the staff to prepare an exact list of what had been stolen.

At that moment, however, no one could have dreamed that Henry Newman was lying in the accident ward of a hospital less than three-hundred kilometres away. His car had skidded on a patch of oil on the road, and he had crashed into a tree.

When the local police searched his car they found the two suitcases and at once suspected that the goods were stolen.

... studded	– ... besetzt(e)
tiepin	– Schlipsnadel
to help oneself	– sich bedienen
to rearrange	– in Ordnung bringen
displays	– Auslagen
to rifle	– ausplündern
sales staff	– Verkaufspersonal
ward	– Abteilung
to skid	– rutschen, schleudern

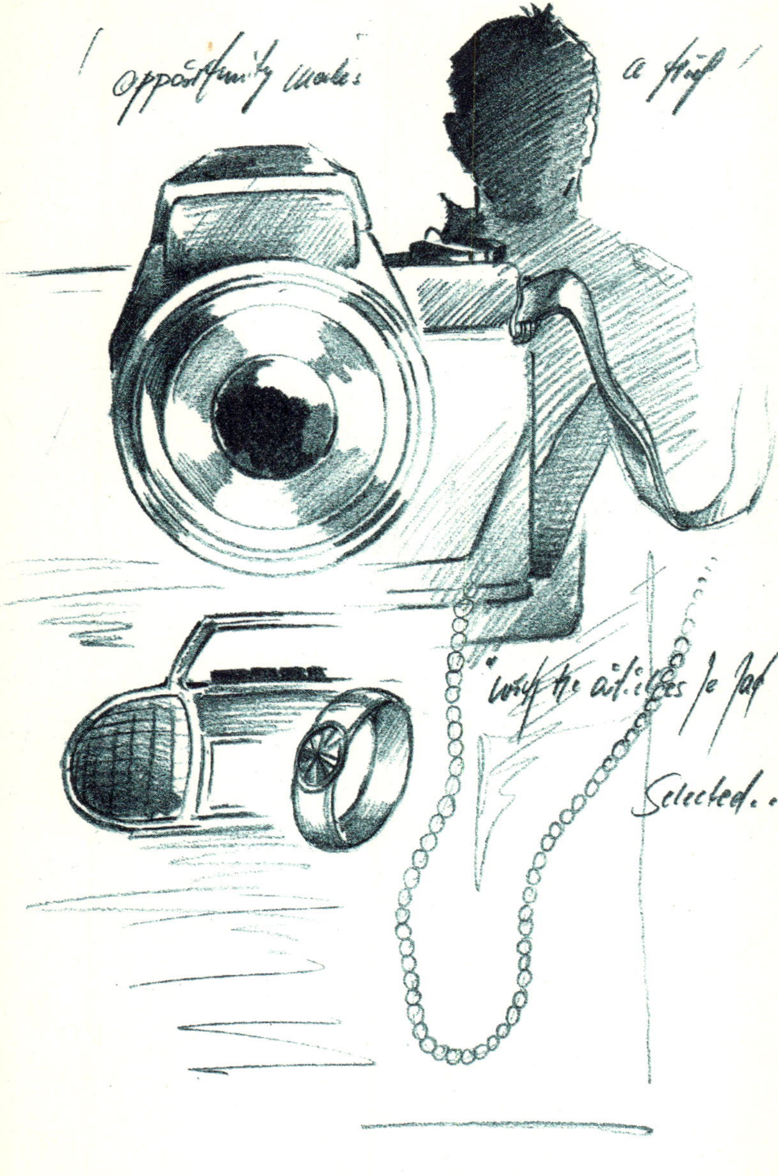
"Opportunity makes a thief"
"Selected..."

But they couldn't question the injured man yet. He was unconscious.

By 11 a.m., the manager of the Great Central Store was in possession of a full list of the missing articles. According to this list, the goods concerned were: eight valuable cameras, two cassette recorders, twelve diamond rings, twenty-four bracelets, four pearl necklaces, six diamond-studded tie-pins, a total of forty-seven wrist watches, ladies' and

to suspect	– vermuten
unconscious	– bewusstlos

men's, three pairs of binoculars, a microscope, and three cigarette-cases.

The manager was horrified at the extent of the theft, but he was relieved when, at about 3 p.m., he received a phone call from the police, telling him that the thief had been found and was now in custody. Furthermore, all the objects taken had been retrieved, undamaged. Before the day was over, the police returned them to the store just as the thief had packed them into his two suitcases.

However, two days later one of the shop's assistants was dismissed without notice, and all because of this robbery.

The question is: in which department did the dismissed assistant work and why was he dismissed?

to be horrified	– bestürzt sein
extent	– Ausmaß, Umfang
to be relieved	– erleichtert sein
furthermore	– weiterhin, des Weiteren
to retrieve	– wiederfinden
to dismiss	– entlassen
without notice	– auf der Stelle, fristlos

4 The sneak-thief

Andrew Harris, head of a department at the Ministry of Defence, had a careless habit: he always left his jacket over the back of his armchair. He did this day in, day out, without a thought for what was in its pockets.

He did this, as usual, on the morning of 1 June. It was a hot day in early summer, a day when Harris' wallet contained no less than fifteen £10 notes.

At 10.05 a.m., Andrew Harris, whose office was on the eighth floor, opened the door of the adjoining room. His secretary rushed to get her notebook, but Mr Harris shook his head. "If you need me: I'll be having a quick word with Mr Abraham. I'll leave this door open, Miss Bush."

"Very well, Sir." At 10.10, Harris – shirt-sleeves rolled up and tie comfortably loosened – left his office by the other door.

At 10.14 he came back to fetch a photograph from his wallet. It was a picture of his four-week-old twins, Jenny and Jeremy.

Andrew Harris took out the photograph and he was already

sneak-thief	– Gelegenheitsdieb
Ministry of Defence	– Verteidigungsministerium
wallet	– Brieftasche
to contain	– enthalten
adjoining	– anschließend, benachbart
shirt-sleeves	– Hemdsärmel

slipping the wallet back into his inside pocket before he realized something was missing. He took out the wallet again and opened it. There was no doubt about it – all his money had gone.

At first he could only shake his head. Then he went to the open door that led to Miss Bush's room.

"Tell me, Miss Bush. Who's been in my room during the last two or three minutes?"

Olga Bush looked puzzled. "In – in – y – your room?" she stammered.

"Yes, in my room."

"No one, Sir."

"But someone *must* have been."

Olga shook her head decidedly. "No one's been in, Mr Harris. I'd have heard them. What makes you ask?" "All the money in my wallet has disappeared. If you didn't hear anyone, with the door open all the time, the thief can't have made any noise at all."

Olga Bush was so appalled she thought she was going to faint. But Andrew Harris sprang into action. He pressed a button which automatically closed all the doors from the fifth floor downwards. At the same time the three house-detectives were alerted, also automatically.

to realize	– bemerken, wahrnehmen
decidedly	– entschieden, entschlossen
appalled	– entsetzt
to faint	– ohnmächtig werden
to spring into action	– handeln
to alert	– hier: alarmieren

By 10.22, a man on the seventh floor aroused suspicion because of one most unusual fact. He was detained, together with two other strangers who were spotted within the next seven minutes. After half an hour, two of the three suspects were allowed to go. The third, however, was handed over to the police within the hour. There was no doubt that he alone had taken the money.

Now Super Sleuths, here's a list of what these three men were wearing and what they carried on them. From this information you should be able to discover which of the three men was the thief.

to arouse suspicion	– Verdacht erwecken
to detain	– festhalten
to spot	– ausmachen, (auf-)finden

Suspect A

Anthony Burton: Dark blue suit of best quality, white shirt, blue tie with white dots, white underwear, short blue socks, black shoes, umbrella, briefcase with some papers, and two packets of assorted tablets for various aches and pains.
In his pockets were a key-ring with six keys, two handkerchiefs, one white and blue, the other plain white, a wallet with £170 in £10 notes, various pens and pencils, a pocket-watch, and a leather-bound notebook.

Suspect B

Ernest Ullmann: Chocolate-brown suit, beige shirt, brown and yellow tie with a tiepin, white underwear, brown woollen patterned socks, briefcase with various papers, including a street plan of the town, and a writing set.
In his pockets were a leather key-wallet containing three keys, a handkerchief, a wallet with £190, including fifteen £10 notes, a pocket-knife and some change.

Suspect C

Oscar Winter: Navy-blue suit, white roll-neck sweater, navy-blue suede shoes, white socks, white underwear, a thin briefcase containing assorted leaflets, dark gloves.

underwear	– Unterwäsche
briefcase	– Aktentasche
assorted	– sortiert, zusammengestellt
change	– Wechselgeld
suede	– Wildleder
leaflet	– Prospekt

In his pockets were a key-ring with a medallion and four keys, a handkerchief, a wallet containing £166, among them sixteen £10 notes, a stop-watch, a pair of scissors in a leather case, a chestnut (he was carrying it to prevent rheumatism), and a miniature pack of cards.

Which one of these three was the wanted man?

chestnut	– Kastanie
to prevent	– fern halten; verhindern

5 The brainwave of the century

Gaston Berlieu, known to the Paris police as an underworld gangster, ran up the stairs of 48 rue Cherbienne two at a time.

At the fourth floor he stopped and rang a door-bell over which was pinned a card: D. BERLIEU.

It took a good three minutes before a sleepy female voice asked: "Who's there?"

"It's me, your brother," called Gaston. "Come on, Dominique. Open up."

A chain rattled, the door opened a crack and the man in the checked jacket, the black shirt, and shrieking yellow tie slipped inside.

"It's three o'clock in the morning!" protested Dominique, who was twenty-three and Gaston's only sister. "Couldn't you have come earlier? First you vanish for weeks on end and then you arrive in the small hours when decent people are fast asleep." She chained the door and shuffled back to her bedroom.

Gaston followed her, smiling, not in the least put out by her

brainwave	– Geistesblitz
crack	– Spalt
checked	– kariert
shrieking yellow	– grellgelb
small hours	– frühe Morgenstunden
decent	– anständig
to shuffle	– schlurfen

outburst. He dropped into an armchair as the girl jumped back into bed.

"What's up with you, disturbing my sleep like this?"

"I've got some news for you," replied Gaston.

Dominique pulled a face. "I know your kind of news! Last time it was that you had to lie low for at least two months."

"But that was ages ago," Gaston protested .

The girl punched her pillow. "It's less than six months ago," she corrected him with a sigh. "But out with it then. What *is* your news?"

"I've been working!"

"What? You?"

Gaston tapped his forehead: "Brainwork!"

"Really? And what's the result?" It was clear from her tone that she did not have a high opinion of her brother's intelligence. But Gaston seemed sure of himself.

"You'll be surprised when I tell you. I've been thinking of all the nice things you've always wanted. First of all, the most elegant fur coat you can buy in Paris. Then we'll throw out all this rubbish" – and here he waved his hand to include everything in the room – "and we'll refurnish it from top to bottom: carpets, classy furniture, chandeliers,

to disturb	– stören
to lie low	– untertauchen
to punch	– schlagen auf
pillow	– Kopfkissen
fur coat	– Pelzmantel
rubbish	– Kram, Plunder
chandeliers	– Leuchter

tablelamps ... And to crown it all the biggest colour TV we can find. I'll buy myself a new car, and if you like we'll still be able to afford a few weeks' holiday in Switzerland. Isn't that something?"

Dominique hardly knew whether to laugh, cry, or send for the doctor! However, as her brother looked in pretty good health she decided to tease the story out of him. "Yes, it really *is* something – if it's true," she answered, yawning.

Her brother stretched out his arms and laughed dramatically. "I'm about to bring off a stroke of genius, the brainwave of the century." Then he explained his brilliant plan. "I don't have to tell you that the police know I only work in white gloves."

Dominique nodded.

"And they also know I smoke nothing but English cigars and that I always use *Elegance* aftershave."

The girl nodded again.

"Well then," he said and paused.

"Well then what?" she snapped.

Gaston Berlieu sat up, straightened his back, threw out his chest, and whispered as gravely as a clergyman: "Tomorrow night, I'm going to clean out Jules Martinique's."

to afford	– sich leisten
to tease out	– herauslocken
to bring off	– zustande bringen, „vom Stapel lassen"
stroke of genius	– Geniestreich
to snap	– schnappen; (bissig) entgegnen
to straighten	– gerade machen; sich aufrichten

"You mean the big jeweller's?" asked Dominique incredulously, her eyes growing larger.

"The jeweller's," Gaston confirmed solemnly.

"No!" gasped Dominique.

"Yes!" answered Gaston. "I know how to switch off the burglar alarm there, and when I've cleared them out I'll spray some *Elegance* around, leave behind my white gloves, a half-smoked Virginia, and my driving licence. Yes, I intend to leave them all deliberately."

Dominique gulped, appalled, but Gaston only laughed. "The day before yesterday I went to report to the police that my driving licence had been stolen."

"But with all those clues they'll be sure it's you! Gloves, aftershave, English cigars ... You may as well phone the police and tell them all about it." She was sneering now; she already had visions of herself carrying food parcels to Gaston in prison.

Gaston's face wore a superior smile. "That's just the point!"

"What point?"

"The brainwave of the century! Even the most stupid policeman will think someone must be trying to frame me!"

incredulous	– ungläubig
to confirm	– bestätigen
solemn	– feierlich
deliberately	– absichtlich
to gulp	– schlucken
clue	– Hinweis, entscheidender Punkt
to sneer	– spotten, feixen
superior	– überlegen
to frame	– nachmachen, nachahmen

It took several minutes for Dominique to understand. "Yes, you're right," she conceded admiringly.
Gaston was still smiling as he kicked off his shoes and announced that he was going to get a few hours' sleep on the sofa.

1.45 a.m. The night-watchman had just passed. Gaston Berlieu slipped on his white gloves and started picking the first

to concede	– zugeben
to pick a lock	– ein Schloss knacken

lock. Twelve minutes later he had reached the elegant showroom and quickly made a clean sweep. All in all, the pieces of jewellery and precious stones he pocketed must have been worth half a million francs at the very least.
Then Berlieu began 'planting' his clues. He squirted his favourite aftershave in all directions. He 'lost' his driving licence between two chairs. He stubbed out the half-smoked English cigar in an expensive ashtray. After that he took off his white gloves and with an ironic bow put them on a showcase, immediately below a large portrait of the founder of the firm. His final gesture was to take down a small **Thank You** sign from the back of the door and lean it against a Chinese vase that he lifted from the floor and placed on the counter.

At 3.30 a.m. he was safely back at 48 rue Cherbienne, where his sister was waiting nervously for him. "Well, what happened?"
Gaston emptied his pockets onto the kitchen table. Rings, necklaces, brooches, watches, gold bracelets, and diamonds, it was a dazzling display, and Dominique, who worked in a sweetshop, saw that Gaston had done exactly what he had promised. Their dreams were coming true!

to make a clean sweep	– gründlich aufräumen
precious stone	– Edelstein
to plant one's clues	– seine Kennzeichen hinterlassen
to squirt	– spritzen
dazzling	– verwirrend, hinreißend
display	– (Waren-)Auslage

"I hope you were careful."
"It went like clockwork."
"That's what you said last time – and the judge gave you three years."
"No, I mean it this time. It worked out perfectly. There's not a thing to worry about," he assured her, stowing away the stolen loot under a loose floorboard. Then he stretched out on the sofa and immediately fell asleep, a contented smile on his lips.

There was a ring at the doorbell at 8.38 that same morning. "See who it is," murmured Gaston, only half awake. Then

judge	– Richter
loot	– Beute

he rolled over to go to sleep again. But seconds later he was woken up roughly by the clattering of – a pair of handcuffs! And the person clapping them on him was none other than Inspector Dupont. He was accompanied, as usual, by his short assistant, Henri Dacot, who was grinning broadly.

"Upon my word, a very amusing idea of yours, Berlieu. I didn't think you had it in you!" smiled Dupont almost cordially. "And if it weren't for one stupid and totally unnecessary slip, I really would have believed some other villain was trying to frame you!"

What had been Gaston's mistake?

cordial	– herzlich
and if it weren't for …	– und wenn da nicht … gewesen wäre
slip	– Fehler; Panne

A question of weight 6

There were four of them.
Emil drove the van, while the three others, the brothers Bill and Tony, and Albert, who was always known as Al, crouched in the back. They were discussing the job ahead.
"I've seen a lot of funny things in my time," Al was saying, "but nothing like this before."
Bill nodded. "I bet it weighs a ton, too."
Tony agreed with his brother. "I wonder what's the idea, pinching something so heavy? What's the chap going to do with it anyway?"
Al scratched his unshaven chin. "Perhaps he collects them – unless there's more to it than meets the eye."
"What d'you mean? How can there be?"
But Al's idea seemed to have faded, for he suddenly thought of something else. "My mum wanted me to learn it when I was a boy. Yes, she had grand ideas for me in those days!"
At that moment, a police siren was heard in the distance, and the three villains ducked automatically.
But they were lucky this time. The patrol wasn't after them.

to crouch	– kauern, hocken
ahead	– hier: der vor ihnen lag
to pinch	– hier: stehlen, klauen
to scratch	– kratzen
unshaven	– unrasiert
than meets the eye	– als man zunächst glaubt
to fade	– verschwinden

Ten minutes later, the van slowed down. It was now five to one in the morning.
Emil switched off the lights and drove into a narrow side-street. He stopped in front of a gate behind which was the large asphalt playground of the school.
Bill's nimble fingers needed only seconds to pick the lock, and the gate swung back silently.

At ten past one, the main door to the building had also been forced open.
Emil tossed some strong carrying-straps to the others.
"What'll we do if the caretaker raises the alarm?" muttered Al.
"Don't worry. I've been told he sleeps like a log," said Emil, dismissing Al's fears.
"Where's the hall?" asked Tony.
"On the first floor," replied Emil.
One behind the other they crept noiselessly up the stone stairs. The door to the hall was unlocked.
"There it is! Let's hope it isn't as heavy as it looks."
"Two hundred and thirty kilograms," murmured Emil.
Al gave a cry of dismay. With his bad back – he'd been in

nimble	– flink
straps	– Gurte
caretaker	– Hausmeister
to raise alarm	– Alarm schlagen
to dismiss	– hier: verscheuchen
dismay	– Entsetzen

bed with it for most of last week – how was he supposed to lift his share of about a hundredweight?

"Sssh!" hissed Emil. "D'you want to wake everybody?"

Clumsily the men fixed the straps they had brought with them.

"One ... two ... three!"

Groaning and panting, the four men tugged and pulled, dragging along their haul.

It took them almost twenty minutes to get it down the stairs and into the yard. When at last it was safely inside the van,

to be supposed to	– sollen
share	– Anteil
clumsy	– unbeholfen
to tug	– ziehen, schleppen
haul	– Fang, Beute

Al was so relieved that he lifted its lid. "Shall I?" he asked mischievously.

Before anyone could answer, Emil made an appalling discovery: all four tyres were as flat as pancakes. It could only mean one thing. Something, somewhere, had gone seriously wrong.

Before the four burglars could find out what it was, four policemen appeared as if from nowhere. And with them was the caretaker, Harry, the one who was supposed to have been sleeping like a log. But there was worse to come: urged on by the cheers and laughter of the police officers, Emil, Bill, Tony, and Al had to return what they had stolen and carry it back up the stairs and into the hall.

What was it that the four brothers had tried to steal?

mischievous(ly)	– boshaft
tyre	– Reifen
there was worse to come	– es sollte noch schlimmer kommen
to urge	– drängen, anfeuern

7 The master plan

David Campbell, who lived in London, was an agent for the Silver Star Insurance Company. He had planned everything carefully in advance. His first step was to send Linda, his wife, and their daughters, Elizabeth and Shirley, into the country, where his parents-in-law lived. That was on Friday evening.

On Saturday, he took all the money he had left, £150 in cash, from the wall-safe in the room he used as his office, and then left the house.
When Campbell returned home from the races at six o'clock that evening, these £150, like all the rest of his money, had been spent gambling at the horse-races. David Campbell was bankrupt.
Calmly he set about putting into effect the second part of his master plan, devised for just this contingency. He used a small but precisely calculated dynamite charge to blow

agent	– Vertreter
insurance company	– Versicherungsgesellschaft
in advance	– im Voraus
parents-in-law	– Schwiegereltern
race	– (Pferde-)Rennen
to put into effect	– verwirklichen
to devise	– ersinnen, ausdenken
contingency	– (unvorhergesehener) Fall
dynamite charge	– Sprengladung

"The Master-plan"

open the office wall-safe. Then he emptied drawers, cupboards, shelves, and business files onto the floor. He also ripped the phone from its socket.
When it was dark, he put on a pair of rubber boots that had a strongly marked pattern on the soles. The boots were three sizes too big for him.
Next he switched off all the lights and went out into the garden. For five minutes he tramped up and down, making certain that he had left enough footprints, before shattering a window in the kitchen door with a stone.
He then entered the house, making sure there was plenty of soil clinging to his boots. He walked down the hall into the office, again leaving plenty of footprints and traces of soil. He returned the way he had come, took off his boots outside, and re-entered the house in his stockings.
With a sharp knife he cut up the rubber boots into small pieces and flushed them down the lavatory.
At 11 p.m. he went and changed into his pyjamas, lay down in bed, tossed and turned, got up again, and stood there

file	– (Akten-)Ordner
to rip	– hier: herausreißen
socket	– Fassung, (Steck-)Dose
boot	– Stiefel
to shatter	– einschlagen
to make sure	– sichergehen, dass ...
soil	– Erde, Erdboden; Dreck
to flush down	– hinunterspülen
lavatory	– Toilette

thinking for a long time. Was he having doubts as to whether or not his master plan was really foolproof? No!
From the drawer of his bedside table he took out a revolver and tiptoed down into the hall, barefoot. From there he fired three shots onto the stairs leading to the bedrooms. A hundred and twenty seconds later he fired again twice, this time from the staircase down into the hall.
It was now 11.11 p.m.
In the bathroom, Campbell smeared a little bit of facecream on his face und sprinkled it with water. He also saw to it that his pyjama jacket was damp, back and front.
David Campbell hoped very much that his neighbours weren't hard of hearing.
At last! At 11.18 he heard the siren of a police patrol car. At 11.22, three police officers came running into the house through the kitchen door. At 11.35, detective sergeant Newton appeared in person, and a trembling David Campbell, bathed in 'sweat', made the following statement:

"There's not much I can say. I had been in bed some time when I was roused by a dull thud. Then I heard noises from the ground floor. I got out my revolver and decided to creep downstairs. From the

foolproof	– idiotensicher
damp	– feucht
back and front	– hinten und vorne
hard of hearing	– schwerhörig
statement	– Aussage
to be roused	– aufgeschreckt werden
dull thud	– dumpfer Schlag

half-landing I suddenly saw a shadow. I called out: 'Stop, or I'll fire!' Then there were three loud bangs. They had shot at me three times. I fired back twice. At this, the shadow vanished into the kitchen. I tried to phone but the line was cut. £15,000 in cash and £10,000 in securities were stolen from my safe."

half-landing	– Treppenabsatz
line	– hier: Kabel
in securities	– in Wertpapieren

When Campbell had signed his statement, Barry Hyde, who had been examining the footprints in the garden, came indoors.
"It's plain as daylight, Jack," he told Newton. "The fellow entered through the garden and the kitchen door. We've taken two casts of the prints made by his boots, und we've fingerprints, too. Whether or not they belong to the culprit we'll have to find out."
While Newton went into the office with Campbell, Hyde got to work extracting the five bullets from the walls of the staircase and the hall.

At forty minutes past midnight that Sunday morning, the officers left the apparently distraught Mr David Campbell. Part two of his master plan had succeeded.
It was getting on for eleven o'clock that same Sunday morning when Campbell had a second visit from detective sergeant Newton. Only this time the man from Scotland Yard was not nearly as sympathetic and friendly.
"Please get dressed immediately and pack a small case with all you'll need. We're taking you to headquarters, and our

cast	– Ausguss
culprit	– Schuldige(r)
to extract	– herausziehen
bullet	– Kugel
apparently distraught	– offensichtlich zu Tode erschreckt
headquarters	– Hauptquartier, Zentrale

talks there may take some time. You have a lot of questions to answer about faking this robbery and break-in."

Campbell nodded wearily and began to dress. He knew when he was beaten. But no matter how hard he racked his brains, he couldn't think what was the mistake he had made in his master plan. What on earth was it?

What was David Campbell's careless mistake?

to fake	– vortäuschen
to rack one's brain	– angestrengt nachdenken, den Kopf zerbrechen

8 The house of the ninety-nine ghosts

Several years ago William Russell, who owned a Glasgow travel company, first had the profitable idea of organizing luxury holidays on the Isle of Skye in the Inner Hebrides. At first, almost all those interested were fellow Scots from the north and east of the country as far as Aberdeen. Then English people got to know about the holidays, and they were later joined by Scandinavians, French, Swiss, Austrians, and people from other European and even overseas countries.

William Russell established many holiday centres, and he used his lively imagination to ensure that the holidaymakers were never bored. There were walking tours, pony trekking, golf matches, angling competitions, and excursions.

However, the high spot of all the entertainments was always the Pirate Safari. It was a sea trip in a converted cutter to

travel company	– Reiseagentur
profitable	– einträglich
Hebrides	– Inseln vor der Westküste Schottlands
fellow Scots	– schottische Landsleute
to establish	– einrichten, gründen
lively imagination	– rege Fantasie
to ensure	– sicherstellen
to bore	– langweilen
competition	– Wettbewerb
high spot	– Höhepunkt
entertainment	– Unterhaltung, Darbietung
converted cutter	– umgebauter Kutter

some of the many islands of the Hebrides, and it was of special interest to keen photographers.

⊙

The situation on 18 September, the date on which this story begins, was this. The season was almost over, and the tourists on Skye were thinning out. All the same, on that September morning Captain Ernest Gilroy had enough passengers for the usual Pirate Safari, and at 8.30 a.m. the *Fortune* was ready to sail. Gilroy, a white-haired stocky man with a squarish head, was sixty-seven and had been a sailor for more than forty years until he became the *Fortune's* captain. In addition to his experience and seamanship he also had the gift of the gab, so he acted as guide and courier as well.

Apart from Captain Gilroy and his crew, the engineer Dick Watson and the deckhand Johnny Beasley, there were nine tourists on board the *Fortune*.

They were:

Eleanor Benfort, fifty-nine, an American who wore spectacles, a blonde wig und bright pink lipstick. She always carried three cameras, and she was amused by anything.

⊙→ to thin out	– weniger werden
stocky	– stämmig
squarish	– quadratisch, eckig
the gift of the gab	– ein gutes Mundwerk
deckhand	– Matrose
wig	– Perücke

She couldn't say a sentence without laughing, even one as ordinary as: "Isn't the sea nice and calm today!"

Henry O'Brien, twenty-six, the owner of a chemist's shop in London. He said little and watched everything. The other tourists looked down on the young man because he was so badly dressed. O'Brien seemed to prefer sitting by himself in the bows of the *Fortune*, staring at the sea ahead.

Paul Pickles, sixty-three, an ex-book-keeper from Birmingham. He glowered at everything, continually chewed on a matchstick, and his few words were spoken in a deep bass voice. He gave the impression that he would never have been on this trip if it had not been for his wife, *Mary Pickles* (maiden name Woodley), aged sixty-one. Mary had a high-pitched voice and she never stopped taking pictures. "Oh look, Paul!" she kept calling, and her camera would click for the umpteenth time.

Ethel Hand, fifty-one, from Canada. She spoke English with a French accent, and she smiled at everyone. She said that she worked as a cashier in a big store, that she had been married twice, and that she was a member of a small religious sect.

chemist's shop	– Apotheke, Drogerie
bow	– Bug, Spitze
to glower at	– finster anblicken
to chew	– kauen
if it had not been for his wife	– wenn nicht seine Frau gewesen wäre
high-pitched	– schrill
for the umpteenth time	– zum x-ten Mal
cashier	– Kassierer(in)

Abraham Mall, forty-nine, a greengrocer, who, like O'Brien, came from London. He walked with a stick and dragged his left leg. He carried a camera.

Maud Canfield, seventy, a widow. She was the only one present who had a video camera and she made good use of it. She came from Worcester.

Jonas Coxley, the same age as Mall, drove his own taxi in Dover, where he lived. Apart from an enormous appetite, his other notable characteristic was a more or less constant

to drag – nachziehen
video camera – Videokamera
notable – bemerkenswert

hiccup. It was a noisy business, and something that *Tommy Lester* in particular seemed to dislike, for he kept shaking his head at Coxley's unfortunate affliction. Lester, sixty-two, was the last of the party on board the *Fortune*. His home was in Wimbledon, but he had lived most of his life in India.

So this was the mixed bunch of passengers who found themselves aboard the *Fortune* on that cool September morning.

Towards ten o'clock, a fresh breeze sprang up. The sea was covered with little crests of foam. The *Fortune* pitched a little, but not very much.

It was at 10.28 that Mary Pickles snapped her twenty-eighth seagull, and Paul, her husband, spat his twelfth matchstick into the Atlantic. At 10.30, Jonas Coxley dug his teeth into the third sandwich since they had left Skye.

Punctually at 11 a.m. they reached the first island of their tour.

In spite of all its charm, the island proved uneventful, and the same must be said of the other stops on the way to their destination.

hiccup	– Schluckauf
affliction	– Heimsuchung, Unglück
crest of foam	– Schaumspitze
to pitch	– schlingern
to snap	– fotografieren
to dig, dug, dug	– graben
in spite of	– trotz
to prove	– sich erweisen als
uneventful	– langweilig
destination	– Ziel(ort)

By now it was afternoon, and at last the *Fortune* was approaching the island of Benmore. As the island came into sight, Captain Gilmore addressed the passengers. "Ladies and gentlemen!" he announced (not without a sideways glance at the shabby O'Brien, as if he didn't really include him in this category): "We are now approaching Benmore, an island I'm sure you've never heard of."

Mary Pickles nodded eagerly at this and squeaked: "I've never heard of it, for one!" The others, too, confirmed Gilroy's statement – except, that is, for Coxley, who was busy holding his breath.

"You all know we call this sea trip the Pirate Safari," the captain went on, "and of course Mr Russell had something definite in mind when he gave it that name. Well, Benmore is the reason for it. We are now coming to one of the most notorious pirate port in these waters, and one that dates from the seventeenth century."

"Is there anything to film there?" asked Mrs Canfield, while Eleanor Benfort laughed: "Oh, pirates! We had them in America, too – particularly in the Caribbean. Ha! ha! ha!"

Ernest Gilroy nodded coolly. "Of course, madam. Where *weren't* there pirates?" And turning to Mrs Canfield, he

to include	– einbeziehen
to squeak	– quieken, piepsen
I ... for one	– ich für meinen Teil
something definite	– etwas Bestimmtes
notorious pirate haven	– berüchtigter Piratenhafen
Caribbean	– Karibische See

said: "You'll find plenty of pictures here, Mrs Canfield. I'm sure you'll get your money's worth. Benmore is uninhabited, but it has one of the most imposing buildings that exist within a radius of several hundred sea miles. It's known as **the house of the ninety-nine ghosts**."

Eleanor Benfort looked up, interested.

Henry O'Brien stared in the direction of the island, unimpressed.

Paul Pickles looked sceptical.

Mary Pickles seemed nervous.

Maud Canfield frowned and retied the scarf round her neck a little more tightly.

Abraham Mall smiled uneasily.

Jonas Coxley had another fit of hiccups.

At last Tommy Lester spoke. "Ghosts?" he echoed.

"Yes, ghosts! Ninety-nine, to be precise." Captain Gilroy uttered the words gravely. "I'll tell you the whole story.

In the days when pirates were the scourge of the high seas, a large ship, the *Devil's Arrow*, was lying at anchor here in the bay of Benmore. It was a pirate ship with a hundred men on board. The captain, whose real name was Nicholas

uninhabited	– unbewohnt
unimpressed	– unbeeindruckt
to retie	– wieder fester machen, ziehen
uneasy	– unbehaglich, ängstlich
fit	– Anfall
scourge	– Geißel

Olding, was known as Nick the Knife. For a bloodthirsty pirate, he was very considerate towards his men, and he had a great house built on Benmore in which to shelter his crew during the notorious November storms.

"What Nick the Knife didn't know was that among the fellows who served him was a traitor. His name was Donald Dale – a man who had made up his mind that the large reward offered by the king for Olding's capture would be his. His plan was simple. At dawn, on 19 August, when Nick the Knife was returning to Benmore, the *Devil's Arrow* was particularly heavily laden. For he had plundered a Portuguese galleon, an English merchantman, and a three-master bound for home from India. It took the pirates more than eleven hours simply to unload all their loot and carry it up to the house.

"That evening, Nicholas Olding arranged a grand feast, and the fine Portuguese wines they had captured should be a reward for his men's drudgery at sea.

Donald Dale saw that his moment had come. Shortly after midnight he put his plan into action. He slipped out of the house, where most of his comrades were already drunk. He

considerate	– aufmerksam, besorgt
to shelter	– Zuflucht, Schutz geben
traitor	– Verräter
reward	– Belohnung
capture	– Gefangennahme
merchantman	– Handelsschiff
bound for ...	– auf der Fahrt nach ...
wine	– Wein
drudgery	– Plackerei, Strapazen

ran as fast as he could the seven hundred metres to the shore, where three pirates had been ordered to keep vigil. "You can go up to the house now and join in the celebrations," he called to them. "I've come to relieve you." He didn't have to tell them twice. Before he could recover his breath the three had disappeared along the path, shouting with joy. Dale lost no time and got down to work. First he set fire to all the rowing boats except one, a three-seater. Then he rowed out in this to the *Devil's Arrow*, which was lying at anchor in the bay, unguarded, three hundred metres from the shore. He climbed on board up the rope ladder and laid an eight metre fuse from the powder-room to the deck. When he had put a light to the fuse, he hurried back to his boat and began to row like fury.

"But for some unknown reason the fuse burned more quickly than he expected. Donald Dale was less than two hundred metres from the big ship when it blew up and began to blaze. The force of the explosion was so great that Dale was flung into the sea. He was able to climb back into the boat but – and this was his great misfortune – the blast had also flung the two oars into the water.

celebrations	– Feierlichkeiten
to recover one's breath	– wieder zu Atem kommen
unguarded	– unbewacht
fuse	– Zündschnur
powder-room	– (Schieß-)Pulvermagazin
like fury	– wie verrückt
to fling (flung, flung)	– schleudern
blast	– (Wind-, Explosions-)Stoß

"Long after the *Devil's Arrow* had sunk, Dale was still paddling with his hands, looking for the lost oars.

"Towards 3 a.m., he was caught in the current and drifted helplessly westwards into the open Atlantic. Twenty-one days later, the crew of a fishing boat rescued him from the sea. Reduced to skin and bone, with a heavy growth of beard and a strange look in his eye, the starving, helpless creature was taken back to Skye, babbling wildly. In spite of every effort, no one could make sense of what he was trying to say. He kept repeating words about a huge bang and a feast, and muttered something about a reward. But he had forgotten his own name, as well as his original plan to sail from the island and betray his own comrades who were stranded on the island.

"It took eleven years for the story to come to light. A fishing boat sprang a leak, and it was almost sinking when it managed to get to Benmore.

"Weeks later, when the fishermen had succeeded in patching up their boat, they returned to Skye, but they had learned what fear meant. And they brought with them not only gold, precious stones and bales of silk, but also three dozen

oar	– Ruder
current	– Strömung
reduced to skin and bone	– bis auf die Knochen abgemagert
to babble	– stammeln, plappern
effort	– Anstrengung
to spring a leak	– ein Leck bekommen
to patch up	– flicken
to mean, meant, meant	– bedeuten

manuscript sheets of paper, from which the world learned about the terrible fate of those marooned on Benmore after Donald Dale had destroyed the *Devil's Arrow* and all the other boats.

The pirates, so it seemed, had been unable to build themselves even a raft, for there are no trees on the island. Their provisions had dwindled from day to day, and after three weeks the last crumbs had been eaten. Dreadful events followed, and all the eight fishermen who returned to Skye swore that the ghosts of the ninety-nine unfortunate pirates

bale of silk	– Ballen von Seide
manuscript sheets	– handgeschriebene Blätter
to maroon	– aussetzen
raft	– Floß
crumb	– Krümel
dreadful	– fürchterlich, furchtbar
event	– Ereignis

still held sway in the great house, and mercilessly haunted every visitor.

Soon the king heard about the affair, and he sent three ships to the island to look for the pirates' plunder. And when the search-party came back, even the most optimistic of those at court were amazed at the riches amassed by Nick the Knife. And to this very day his hide-out has retained its name: **The house of the ninety-nine ghosts**."

⦿

Ernest Gilroy's vivid description produced widely different reactions. "What a name you'd have made for yourself in the East as a storyteller, Captain! Ha! ha! ha!" Eleanor Benfort tried to hide her agitation with her compliment. One could tell at once that she was less at ease than she pretended to be. Mary Pickles, Jonas Coxley, and Maud Canfield also seemed to regret having made the excursion. "What a yarn! I don't believe a word of it!" scoffed Mr Mall, quietly sceptical.

to hold sway	– herrschen
merciless	– gnadenlos
to haunt	– verfolgen
plunder	– Raub, Ware
to amass	– anhäufen, ansammeln
to this very day	– bis zum heutigen Tag
hide-out	– Versteck
vivid	– lebhaft
agitation	– Erregung
to be at ease	– sich wohl fühlen
yarn	– Seemannsgarn; erlogene Geschichte
to scoff	– spotten

Gilroy turned to the speaker, his eyes blazing. "I believe you're from London, Sir, aren't you?"
When the greengrocer nodded, the captain continued: "Then I suggest you pay a visit to the Maritime Museum when you get home. In Room Twelve, on the third floor, you will find a glass case on the right-hand side, and there you will see the actual document written by a certain Octavius Springly."
"Was … was he the … the man who …?" stammered Mall in embarrassment.
"Yes," said Gilroy sternly. "He was the man whose writings were found by the fishermen."
"Hic …" was heard from starboard, followed by yet another "Hic!" Coxley had been seized once more by a fit of hiccups.
"You shouldn't eat so much," snapped Abraham Mall, turning to the taxi-driver from Dover.
"What's it … hic … got to do with you? I'll eat as much as I … hic … please …"
Mrs Canfield too appeared to have thrown off the effects of Gilroy's tale, for she announced defiantly: "I'm going to film the haunted house. I'll never let my grandchildren say that granny was afraid!"
"Then I'll take some photos, too, Paul," piped Mary. Paul

embarrassment	– Verlegenheit
to seize	– packen, ergreifen
defiant(ly)	– trotzig
granny (= grandmother)	– Großmutter

Pickles shifted a matchstick from the left to the right corner of his mouth. "Do as you please," he said, forcing the words from between clenched teeth.

By now the *Fortune* was within a few hundred metres of the small landing-stage, and at exactly 4.30 p.m. she pulled in alongside the quay. Dick Watson and Johnny Beasley tied her up, while the nine passengers, each with different emotions, gazed at the scene, eager to spot any signs of the disaster of three hundred years before.

"So this is where it all happened," mused old Mrs Canfield. She quickly produced her video camera and started filming stones, water, and everything on the shore. Mary Pickles, on the other hand, preferred to take a picture of Dick Watson, who, in her opinion, looked very much as the treacherous Donald Dale had done all those years before.

"And is the island completely uninhabited?" asked Ethel Hand. When Gilroy hesitated, she persisted: "Or isn't it?"

"There is a man on the island who keeps an eye on the house," the captain admitted. However, he did not tell them that during the summer this man was stationed on Benmore for security reasons, and that he was in permanent radio contact with Skye.

to clench	– (zusammen)pressen
to pull in	– anlegen
eager to spot	– begierig zu entdecken
disaster	– Unglück
to muse	– (nach-)sinnen, grübeln
treacherous	– verräterisch
to persist	– beharren
for security reasons	– aus Sicherheitsgründen

Pointing to the east, Gilroy said: "Please follow me to the house. This is the way."
The path before them was overgrown with a thick tangle of plants and bushes. Gilroy led the party slowly, so as not to make things too difficult for the lame Mr Mall. Henry O'Brien and Mrs Hand straggled behind the others. The latter stooped to look at one of the plants, which she plucked.
"Look what's growing here, Mr O'Brien," she exclaimed. "It's incredible, isn't it, at this time of the year and in such a place?" She showed the young man what she had picked, but he seemed uninterested.
"Don't you know what it is?"
He shook his head.
"It's coltsfoot. Do you mean to say you've never heard of it?"
O'Brien shook his head again. "Sorry, Mrs Hand. I don't know much about flowers."
"But it's a very useful herb," she explained. "You use it for infusions and inhaling and many other things." She seemed genuinely shocked at such ignorance.
With a smile, Henry replied. "I hope it's not a crime to be

tangle	– Gewirr, Durcheinander
to straggle	– (hinterher-)bummeln, -zotteln
the latter	– die Letztere
to stoop	– sich bücken
coltsfoot	– Huflattich
herb	– Kraut, Pflanze
inhaling	– Inhalieren, Einatmen

ignorant about things like coltsfoot and their medicinal qualities. And I also hope you won't hold my ignorance against me."

Now it was the Canadian lady's turn to smile. And they had to hurry to catch up with the others.

After rounding a group of tall rocks **the house of the ninety-nine ghosts** unexpectedly came into sight. Huge, massive, stony. Among the pirates must have been a fair number of men who knew something about house building.

For a few seconds the new arrivals stood and stared, remembering vividly what Gilroy had told them about the place and its inhabitants.

But the impression it gave was hardly that of a house more than three hundred years old. The doors and window-frames, in so far as they had been made of wood, had rotted away in the course of time, but the rest looked solid enough.

"Come inside," cried Gilroy. Slowly the others followed him into the main hall, which was a good three hundred and fifty square metres in area and about six metres high. The floor was paved with square stone slabs. A wide staircase led to an upper floor, but admittance to it was barred by nailed planks.

Gilroy addressed the party, and because of the echo he

to catch up with	– einholen, aufholen
a fair number	– eine ganze Anzahl
to pave	– pflastern
slab	– Platte, Fliese
admittance	– Zugang
to bar	– versperren

raised his voice: "It was here in this enormous hall that the pirates must have feasted to celebrate Nicholas Olding's successful raids ... And over there, it is said" – and here he pointed to a recess beside the staircase – "stood a wooden chest containing the Octavius Springly papers I have mentioned, recording the terrible fate of the ninety-nine pirates ... When the wind rises, the house comes to life ..." Gilroy nodded here, as if in affirmation of his own words. "And then the ghosts start singing."

Mary Pickles shuddered.

There was a long silence, and again Tommy Lester was the first to break it. He looked serious and self-important. "Ah yes," he nodded. "The Wind Demons. I've often heard them in India."

"Wind Demons?" Mrs Benfort swallowed hard.

"Yes," said Lester. "They lurk in every corner. Sometimes in old ruines it sounds fantastic, like a ghost symphony ..."

Paul Pickles spat out his matchstick impatiently. "Nonsense!" he grumbled in his deepest bass voice. "It's only the wind whistling or the storm howling. The rest is poppycock!"

raid	– Raubzug, Überfall
recess	– Winkel, Nische
affirmation	– Bestätigung
self-important	– wichtigtuerisch
lurk	– lauern
to grumble	– grollen, murren
poppycock	– Quatsch, dummes Zeug

4.55 p.m

"Ladies and gentlemen, you have another quarter of an hour in which to take pictures. In exactly fifteen minutes from now we shall all reassemble here." Before the nine passengers could answer Gilroy had disappeared with a cheerful wave of his hand.

4.56 p.m. Those who had brought cameras with them started taking photographs, and Mary Pickles was especially keen.

4.58 p.m. Eleanor Benfort was picking up a small stone not far from the barred staircase when her glance fell on the door. She dropped the stone and let out such a piercing scream that the others froze in their tracks. They turned towards her and the American lady pointed to the entrance, her eyes wide with terror.

"A ghost!" screamed Eleanor, while Mrs Canfield, with great presence of mind, raised her video camera. Who would miss the opportunity of filming a ghost, especially when it looked like this one – wizened and old, with a bald head and a good-natured wrinkled face which now showed obvious signs of excitement. But why shouldn't a ghost get excited sometimes? He was dressed in an old anorak – and

glance	– Blick
piercing	– durchdringend
to freeze in one's track	– wie angewurzelt stehen bleiben
presence of mind	– Geistesgegenwart
wizened	– verhutzelt
bald	– kahl
wrinkled	– faltig

wore spectacles. “I’m Bernie Hampson,” croaked the little man, “and I’m looking for Captain Gilroy. It’s urgent!”
Silence.
Ethel Hand was the first to recover. “He’s left just this minute,” she said. The ghost put his right index finger to his bald head saluting and disappeared ... And like a ghost he left no trace behind.

5 p.m.
In a wooden hut, fifty metres from the pirate’s house, stood Captain Gilroy, his engineer, and his deckhand.
“Wherever has Bernie got to?” asked Captain Gilroy.
“He went out a few moments ago to find you, Sir,” said Watson, surprised.
“Why didn’t I meet him then?”
“I expect he went left round the rocks and you went right.”
“Well that would explain it. Do you know what he wants me for? Has anything happened?”
The two men knew very little. “As we arrived he was taking down a message over the radio. Then he mumbled something that sounded like ‘Gangster!’ and shot out of the door,” reported Beasley.
“Funny!” muttered Gilroy. He hated mysteries.

to croak	– quaken, krächzen
urgent	– dringend
to recover	– zu sich kommen
index finger	– Zeigefinger
to mutter	– murren, murmeln

At that moment, however, the problem was solved, because Bernie Hampson, the wireless operator on the island of Benmore, came in, gesticulating wildly.
"There you are, Cap'n!" He dropped heavily on a chair, breathing hard. "You've a gangster aboard the *Fortune*!" he snorted.
"What? Who says so?"
"An anonymous caller informed the police in Portree, who told the Russell Agency in Bualintur, and they told me – ha!" (He often said "Ha!" when he got excited.)
"What's his name?"
"Hugh Halloway."
Gilroy calmly counted his passengers. "I know the names of all the male tourists. There's O'Brien, Pickles, Mall, Coxley and Lester on this trip – but no one called Halloway."
"I suppose it's possible he's using an assumed name," suggested Hampson.
"Of course. But didn't they give you a personal description, or say how old he is?"
Bernie shook his head.
At that moment – it was 5.02 p.m. precisely – someone who had been eavesdropping on this conversation glided away from the shadow of the hut and disappeared in the direction

wireless operator	– Funker
to snort	– schnauben
male	– männlich
assumed name	– Deckname
to eavesdrop	– lauschen

of the landing-place. It was one of the *Fortune's* passengers. Inside the shed, Captain Gilroy was shrugging helplessly. "Well then, there's nothing I can do about it," he declared at last and, turning to his crew, he asked: "Or do you think I'll get an answer if I ask them: "Which of you answers to the name of Halloway?"

The men shook their heads.

Gilroy turned back to Bernie Hampson. "Didn't those clever dicks in Portree give any instructions?"

"All they said was that you should detain the villain when you get back to Bualintur, and not let him slip ashore."

At this the captain broke into a loud laughter. "They must be half-wits at HQ, silly asses, all of 'em! ... Did you ever hear such nonsense!"

Dick and Johnny were both surprised at their captain. They had never seen him so amused before, and they couldn't imagine what was tickling him so much ... It must have been something very funny indeed to send him off like that. As if he had read their thoughts Gilroy's laughter stopped abruptly. He wiped a tear from his eye and looked at each in turn. "You haven't the faintest idea why I'm so amused, have you now?" he asked, and they admitted that they hadn't.

Gilroy tapped his forehead. "They tell me to detain a fellow,

dick	– Schnüffler, Polizist
ashore	– an Land
halfwit	– Schwachkopf
HQ (headquarters)	– Zentrale, Hauptquartier
to tickle	– amüsieren; kitzeln

and they haven't given me the slightest clue as to who he is nor what he looks like. Isn't that a joke?"

Watson, Beasley, and Hampson had to agree, once it had been explained to them, and they also grinned.

"What's this gangster been up to?" the captain wanted to know.

Bernie turned to a heap of papers.

"I've written it down somewhere. Ha," he mumbled. "Here it is. A man named Hugh Halloway has robbed a bank in Dundee."

"And how much money did he take?"

"They didn't say."

"Was anyone hurt?"

"I don't know that either."

"A fine bunch, our local police!" said Gilroy with disgust. "A fine bunch, I must say!"

After chatting for a moment or two about other things, it was time for Gilroy and his men to fetch the party.

At 5.10 they reached the house of the ninety-nine ghosts. The assembled passengers looked at them expectantly.

"Everyone here?" asked the captain, although it was quite unnecessary, as he could see at a glance that no one was missing.

once …	– nachdem es einmal …
What's he been up to?	– Was hat er angestellt?
bunch	– Haufen, „Verein“
to chat	– reden, sich unterhalten über

"You're as punctual as the 9 o'clock news!" laughed Mr Mall.

"If you want to be back in Skye this evening, we must leave now. Unless, of course, you'd prefer to spend the night in the haunted house." And as Gilroy spoke he studied the five men in the party unobtrusively. Which of them was Hugh Halloway? The quiet Henry O'Brien? He was the youngest, and bank robbers are likely to be young men. What about the book-keeper Pickles? But no, it couldn't be him. He was travelling with his wife, after all. Or was his wife only a cover-up? Perhaps she wasn't really his wife, but an accomplice! What about Abraham Mall, the greengrocer? Or the taxi-driver, Jonas Coxley? Or was Tommy Lester a suspicious character? Who was Hugh Halloway, among these five?

The captain would have to wait and see. Meanwhile, no one wanted to stay on Benmore a moment longer than he had to.

With everyone back on the *Fortune* by 5.23 p.m., Captain Gilroy was waiting for the sound of the diesel engine to start. But no sound came from the engine room. "Watson!" he bawled. "Have you gone to sleep?"

The engineer appeared from down below, his hands covered in oil.

cover-up	– Tarnung
to bawl	– brüllen, grölen

"The blasted engine won't start, Sir," he swore.
Gilroy looked at him reprovingly. "Mr Watson, there are ladies present."
"Sorry, Sir. But all the same, the engine won't start."
"Then find out what's wrong."
"Aye, aye, Sir."

blasted – verflucht
reproving – tadelnd

At 6 p.m. the engineer and Johnny Beasley were still trying to find the fault, and the passengers were becoming increasingly restless. No one wanted to spend the night in the company of ninety-nine ghosts. At last, at a quarter past six, Watson discovered what was wrong. Furiously he reported back to Gilroy: "Someone has cut the main feed – deliberately!" he snorted. "I couldn't possibly have guessed it was anything like that."
"Someone?" repeated the captain. Watson nodded. And both men were thinking the same thing.
"How long will you need to repair it?"
"Oh, it's easy now I've located the trouble. We should be away within ten minutes or so."

At 6.30 p.m. precisely the propeller was whirling away and tossing up clouds of spray. An hour and a half later, Johnny had to light up – green for starboard, red for port. Green on the right and red on the left. For a long time, nothing could be heard except the engine, the gurgling and hissing of the water – and Jonas Coxley's hiccups. Most of the passengers sat huddled against the cold in the quickly gathering darkness.

fault	– Fehler
main feed	– (Haupt-)Treibstoffleitung
to locate	– (heraus-)finden
to light up	– Positionslampen setzen
starboard	– Steuerbord (rechts)
port	– Backbord (links)
huddled	– eingehüllt, eingewickelt

When at last they saw in the distance the small but brightly lit quayside of Bualintur in Skye, they were enormously relieved. Not even the sight of three uniformed policemen leaning casually against their Land Rover gave rise to any special reactions. Except from one passenger – the man cowering aft beside a coil of rope. "Hi, Jess!" shouted Ethel Hand in a voice loud enough to wake the deafest of sleeping seagulls.

"Hi, Ethie!" shouted an equally loud male voice from the quay in response.

"Is that your husband?" asked Mary Pickles in her usual squeak.

"Sure!" nodded the lady from Canada.

By now several more of those on deck had also recognized friends ashore who were waiting for them. Amidst all the waving and calling, no one was aware that one member of that party of nine who had spent the whole day together had slipped silently into the water under cover of darkness.

By now it was a quarter to eleven, and the *Fortune* was within a hundred metres of the quay.

The general astonishment turned into alarm, the alarm into

brightly lit	– hell erleuchtet
casually	– zufällig; unauffällig
to give rise to	– erzeugen, verursachen
to cower	– kauern
aft	– achtern
coil	– Rolle
deaf	– taub
under cover	– unterm Schutz

anger, and the anger into disbelief when the police sprang into action without warning, and it was established that one passenger (of whom meanwhile a precise description had been given) was no longer on board the *Fortune*.
But perhaps it was some compensation to at least a few of them to hear that, two days later, the man in question, sneezing violently, had been found hiding in a barn not far from Bracadale, and was arrested.

But who was the bank robber, whose real name was Hugh Halloway?

Some facts mentioned in this story give precise information.

anger	– Zorn
disbelief	– Unglaube
to establish	– feststellen
compensation	– Entschädigung
to sneeze	– niesen
violent(ly)	– heftig
barn	– Scheune

Solutions

The left-luggage locker thieves

page ⟶ 7

The item was the duplicate key to locker 52. To get the original keys, the thieves first deposited a piece of their own luggage. This thief used one key to get his suitcase from the locker, so the one found in his pockets must have been a duplicate. It was not surprising that the man knew what there was inside his own suitcase!

The film show

page ⟶ 11

As there were five mistakes in the passage, Mike, who said "Seven!", was farthest from the right number, and so he didn't go to the film show. The five mistakes were:

1. In Switzerland, the rent of a flat would be paid in francs, not Marks.
2. Zurich lies on Lake Zurich, not on Lake Lucerne.
3. A one-room flat wouldn't have a living-room, dining-room, and bedroom.
4. Weingold asked two cronies to come to his flat. But three of them – Kurt, Sandy, and Matt – turned up.
5. If Thursday was 14 September, Sunday would have been the seventeenth, not the eighteenth.

⟶ to deposit – (ins Gepäckfach) abstellen

Opportunity makes ...

page → 17

The assistant who was dismissed had worked in the watch department. He had used the occasion of the burglary to steal two watches himself, reporting that forty-seven watches had been stolen, when Henry Newman had taken only forty-five, nineteen men's and twenty-six ladies'. The deception came to light when the police returned the stolen goods to the manager of the store.

The sneak-thief

page → 22

It was Suspect B. He wore no shoes! And who but a sneak-thief would walk through the offices of the Ministry of Defence in his stockinged feet?

The brainwave of the century

page → 28

In his eagerness, Gaston Berlieu slipped off his gloves too soon, and so left his fingerprints on the Chinese vase and on the sign.

A question of weight

page → 37

The solution has a short answer: a piano.

The master plan

page → 42

David Campbell had thought of everything except that, for the experts at Scotland Yard, it was child's play to find out that the bullets did not come from two guns, but that all five shots had been fired from the same revolver.

deception – Betrug

Hugh Halloway was hiding behind the name of Henry O'Brien. Two important details will not have escaped the notice of any Super Sleuths who have read this story carefully.

Henry O'Brien was the owner of a chemist's shop. If that were true, he would certainly have known about coltsfoot as a herb, and that it has medicinal qualities.

The second detail concerns age and distances. At 5.02 p.m., an eavesdropper, who was one of the passengers, glided away from the back of the hut in which Bernie Hampson, the captain, and his crew were discussing the radio message. This unknown person then went down the path to the landing-stage where he sabotaged the engine. Yet when Gilroy returned to the haunted house at 5.10, this same person was already back there with the rest of the party. In other words, he had covered a distance – there and back – of about 1,400 metres, and had also interfered with the *Fortune's* engine, all within a matter of eight minutes. This could only have been done by a young and fit person, and no one but Henry O'Brien answered this description.

to escape	– entgehen
to concern	– betreffen
to cover	– hier: zurücklegen
to interfere (with)	– sich zu schaffen machen (an)
to answer	– hier: passen auf

Vocabulary

A

according to [ə'kɔːdɪŋ]	– entsprechend
adjoining [ə'dʒɔɪnɪŋ]	– benachbart, angrenzend
admittance [əd'mɪtəns]	– Zugang
in advance [əd'vɑːns]	– im Voraus
affirmation [æfə'meɪʃn]	– Bestätigung
affliction [ə'flɪkʃən]	– Heimsuchung, Unglück, Kummer
to afford [ə'fɔːd]	– sich leisten
aft [ɑːft]	– achtern, hinten
agent ['eɪdʒənt]	– Vertreter
agitation [ædʒɪ'teɪʃn]	– Erregung
ahead [ə'hed]	– vorn, voraus(-liegend)
to alert [ə'lɜːt]	– alarmieren
to amass [ə'mæs]	– anhäufen, ansammeln
anger ['æŋgə]	– Zorn, Ärger
to answer ['ɑːnsə]	– antworten hier: passen auf
appalled [ə'pɔːld]	– entsetzt
to arouse [ə'raʊz]	– erwecken
assorted [ə'sɔːtɪd]	– sortiert, zusammengestellt

B

to babble [bæbl]	– stammeln, plappern
bale [beɪl]	– Ballen
barn [bɑːn]	– Scheune
bawl [bɔːl]	– brüllen, grölen
blast [blɑːst]	– Stoß (vom Wind oder Explosion)

blasted [blɑːstɪd]	– verflucht
boot [buːt]	– Stiefel
to bore [bɔː]	– langweilen
to bother with ['bɒðə]	– sich abgeben mit
bound for [baʊnd]	– auf der Fahrt nach
bow [baʊ]	– Bug
bracelet ['breɪslɪt]	– Armband
brainwave ['breɪnweɪv]	– Geistesblitz
briefcase ['briːfkeɪs]	– Aktentasche
bullet ['bʊlɪt]	– (Gewehr-)Kugel
bunch [bʌntʃ]	– Haufen; ‚Verein'

C

capture ['kæptʃə]	– Gefangennahme
caretaker ['keəteɪkə]	– Hausmeister
cashier ['kæʃɪə]	– Kassierer(in)
cast [kɑːst]	– Ausguss
to catch up with [kætʃ]	– einholen
celebrations [selɪ'breɪʃnz]	– Feierlichkeiten
chandelier [ʃændɪ'lɪə]	– Leuchter
charge [tʃɑːdʒ]	– hier: Ladung
to chat [tʃæt]	– reden, sich unterhalten
checked [tʃekt]	– kariert
chemist ['kemɪst]	– Apotheker, Drogist
chestnut ['tʃesnʌt]	– Kastanie
to chew [tʃuː]	– kauen
to clench [klentʃ]	– (zusammen-)pressen
clumsy ['klʌmzɪ]	– unbeholfen
coil [kɔɪl]	– Rolle
coltsfoot ['kəʊltsfʊt]	– Huflattich
company ['kʌmpənɪ]	– Gesellschaft

compensation [kɒmpen'zeɪʃn] – Entschädigung
competition [kɒmpə'tɪʃn] – Wettbewerb
to concede [kən'si:d] – zugeben
to concern [kən'sɜ:n] – betreffen
to confirm [kən'fɜ:m] – bestätigen
considerate [kən'sɪdərɪt] – aufmerksam, besorgt
to contain [kən'teɪn] – enthalten
contents ['kəntents] – Inhalt
contingency [kən'tɪndʒənsɪ] – (unvorhergesehener) Fall
to convert [kən'vɜ:t] – verwandeln
hier: umbauen
cordial ['kɔ:djəl] – herzlich
to cover ['kʌvə] – bedecken,
hier: zurücklegen
to cower ['kaʊə] – kauern
crack [kræk] – Spalt
crest [krest] – Spitze, Kamm
to croak [krəʊk] – quaken, krächzen
crony ['krəʊnɪ] – Kumpel, Kumpan
crook [krʊk] – Gauner
to crouch [kraʊtʃ] – kauern, hocken
crumb [krʌm] – Krümel
culprit ['kʌlprɪt] – Schuldige(r)
currency ['kʌrənsɪ] – Währung, Geld
current ['kʌrənt] – Strömung
custody ['kʌstədɪ] – Gewahrsam

D

damp [dæmp] – feucht
dazzle [dæzl] – verwirren
deaf [def] – taub

decent ['di:sənt]	– anständig
deception [dɪ'sepʃn]	– Betrug
decided(ly) [dɪ'saɪdɪd]	– entschlossen, bestimmt
deckhand ['dekhænd]	– Matrose
defence [dɪ'fens]	– Verteidigung
defiant [dɪ'faɪənt]	– trotzig
definite ['defɪnɪt]	– bestimmt; Bestimmtes
deliberate(ly) [dɪ'lɪbərət]	– absichtlich
department [dɪ'pɑ:tmənt]	– Abteilung
destination [destɪ'neɪʃn]	– Zielort
to detain [dɪ'teɪn]	– festhalten
to devise [dɪ'vaɪz]	– planen, ersinnen
dick [dɪk]	– Schnüffler, Polizist
disaster [dɪ'zɑ:stə]	– Unglück
disbelief [disbə'li:f]	– Unglaube
discovery [dis'kʌvərɪ]	– Entdeckung
dismay [dɪs'meɪ]	– Entsetzen
to dismiss [dɪs'mɪs]	– entlassen; verscheuchen
display [dɪs'pleɪ]	– (Waren-)Auslage
distraught [dɪs'trɔ:t]	– völlig verwirrt, zu Tode erschreckt
to disturb [dɪs'tɜ:b]	– stören
to drag [dræg]	– nachziehen
dreadful ['dredfʊl]	– furchtbar, fürchterlich
drudgery ['drʌdʒərɪ]	– Plackerei, Strapazen
to be due to [dju:]	– zurückzuführen sein

E

eager ['i:gə]	– begierig
to be at ease [i:z]	– sich wohl fühlen
to eavesdrop ['i:vzdrɒp]	– lauschen

effort ['efət]	– Anstrengung
embarrassment [ɪm'bærəsmənt]	– Verlegenheit
to ensure [ɪn'ʃʊə]	– sicherstellen
entertainment [entə'teɪnmənt]	– Unterhaltung, Darbietung
equipment [ɪ'kwɪpmənt]	– Ausrüstung
to escape [ɪs'keɪp]	– entgehen
to establish [ɪ'stæblɪʃ]	– einrichten, gründen; feststellen
to esteem [ɪs'tiːm]	– (hoch) schätzen
event [ɪ'vent]	– Ereignis
extent [ɪks'tent]	– Ausmaß
to extract [ɪks'trækt]	– herausziehen

F

to fade [feɪd]	– verschwinden
to fail [feɪl]	– daneben-, (schief)gehen
to faint [feɪnt]	– ohnmächtig werden
to fake [feɪk]	– vortäuschen
fault [fɔːlt]	– Fehler
feast [fiːst]	– Fest, Feier
file [faɪl]	– (Akten-)Ordner
fit [fɪt]	– Anfall
flat [flæt]	– (Miet-)Wohnung
to fling, flung, flung [flɪŋ, flʌŋ]	– schleudern
to flush down [flʌʃ]	– hinunterspülen
foolproof ['fuːlpruːf]	– idiotensicher
force [fɔːs]	– Gewalt
to forge [fɔːdʒ]	– fälschen
to frame [freɪm]	– nachmachen, nachahmen

fur [fɜː] – Pelz

furthermore [fɜːðəˈmɔː] – des Weiteren, darüber hinaus

fuse [fjuːz] – Sicherung
hier: Zündschnur

G

to gamble [ˈgæmbl] – Glücksspiele machen

gang [gæŋ] – Bande

glance [glɑːns] – Blick

gloves [glʌvz] – Handschuhe

to glower at [ˈglaʊə] – finster anblicken

granny [ˈgrænɪ] = grandmother – Oma, Großmutter

to grumble [ˈgrʌmbl] – grollen

to gulp [gʌlp] – schlucken

H

halfwit [ˈhɑːfwɪt] – Schwachkopf

hard of hearing [ˈhɑːd ɒv ˈhɪəriŋ] – schwerhörig

haul [hɔːl] – Fang, Beute

to haunt [hɔːnt] – verfolgen

headquarters [= HQ] [ˈhedkwɔːtəz] – Hauptquartier, Zentrale

Hebrides [ˈhebrɪdiːz] – Hebriden (schott. Inseln)

to help oneself [hɛlp wʌnˈsɛlf] – sich bedienen

to hesitate [ˈhezɪteɪt] – zögern

hiccup [ˈhɪkʌp] – Schluckauf

hide-out [ˈhaɪdaʊt] – Versteck

high-pitched [ˈhaɪˈpɪtʃt] – schrill

to horrify [ˈhɒrɪfaɪ] – erschrecken; bestürzen

to huddle [ˈhʌdl] – einhüllen, einwickeln

I

imagination [ɪmædʒɪ'neɪʃn] – Fantasie
to include [ɪn'klu:d] – einbeziehen
to increase [ɪn'kri:s] – zunehmen
incredulous [ɪn'kredjʊləs] – ungläubig
inhaling [ɪn'heɪlɪŋ] – Einatmen, Inhalieren
innocense ['ɪnəsəns] – Unschuld
inside out ['ɪnsaɪd 'aʊt] – wie seine Westentasche, in- und auswendig
insurance company [in'ʃʊərəns 'kʌmpənɪ] – Versicherung(sgesellschaft)
to interfere [ɪntə'fɪə] – sich zu schaffen machen
item ['aɪtəm] – Gegenstand, Stück

J

judge [dʒʌdʒ] – Richter

L

landing ['lændɪŋ] – Treppenabsatz
latter ['lætə] – Letztere(r)
lavatory ['lævətərɪ] – Toilette
... -in -law [ɪn lɔ:] – Schwieger…
leaflet ['li:flɪt] – Prospekt
leak [li:k] – Leck, Loch
left-luggage locker ['lɛft 'lʌgɪdʒ 'lɒka] – Gepäckschließfach
line [laɪn] – (Telefon-)Kabel; Leitung
lively ['laɪvlɪ] – lebhaft
to locate [loʊ'keɪt] – (heraus-)finden
lock [lɒk] – Schloss
loot [lu:t] – Beute
loss [lɒs] – Verlust

to lurk [lɜːk] – lauern, (herum-) schleichen

M

to make sure [meɪk ʃʊə] – darauf achten
male [meɪl] – männlich
to maroon [məˈruːn] – aussetzen, allein lassen
merchantman [ˈmɜːtʃəntmən] – Handelsschiff
merciless [ˈmɜːsɪləs] – gnadenlos
mischievous [ˈmɪstʃɪvəs] – boshaft
to muse [mjuːz] – (nach-)sinnen, grübeln
to mutter [ˈmʌtə] – murren; murmeln

N

necklace [ˈneklɪs] – Halsband
nimble [nɪmbl] – flink
notable [ˈnəʊtəbl] – bemerkenswert
without notice [ˈnəʊtɪs] – fristlos
notorious [nəʊˈtɔːrɪəs] – berüchtigt

O

oar [ɔː] – Ruder
opportunity [ɒpəˈtjuːnɪtɪ] – Gelegenheit
owl [aʊl] – Eule

P

particular [pəˈtɪkjʊlə] – besondere(s)
to patch up [pætʃ] – flicken
pattern [ˈpætən] – Muster, Modell; Plan
to pave [peɪv] – pflastern
performance [pəˈfɔːməns] – Vorstellung, Veranstaltung

to persist [pəˈsɪst] – beharren
petty [ˈpetɪ] – unbedeutend, klein

to pick (a lock) [pɪk]	– (Schloss) knacken
piercing [ˈpɪəsɪŋ]	– durchdringend
to pinch [pɪntʃ]	– kneifen, zwicken hier: stehlen, klauen
to pitch [pɪtʃ]	– schlingern
to plunder [ˈplʌndə]	– plündern
poppycock [ˈpɒpɪkɒk]	– Quatsch, dummes Zeug
port [pɔːt]	– Backbord
precious [ˈpreʃəs]	– wertvoll; Edel …
presence of mind [ˈprezɪns əv maɪnd]	– Geistesgegenwart
to pretend [prɪˈtend]	– vortäuschen
to prevent [prɪˈvent]	– verhindern; fern halten
profitable [ˈprɒfɪtəbl]	– Gewinn bringend
to protest [prəˈtest]	– beteuern, protestieren
to prove [pruːv]	– beweisen; sich erweisen als
to provide for [prəˈvaɪd]	– Vorkehrungen treffen
to pull in [pʊl ɪn]	– anlegen
to put into effect (action) [pʊt ˈɪntuː ɪˈfɛkt]	– umsetzen, verwirklichen

Q

to queue [kjuː]	– Schlange stehen

R

race [reɪs]	– Rennen
to rack [ræk] (one's brain)	– martern, anstrengen (den Kopf zerbrechen)
raft [rɑːft]	– Floß

to raise [reɪz]	– (er-)heben; (Alarm) schlagen
to realize ['rɪəlaɪz]	– bemerken, wahrnehmen
to rearrange ['ri:ə'reɪndʒ]	– in Ordnung bringen
to recover [rɪ'kʌvə]	– zu sich kommen
~ (one's breath)	(wieder zu Atem kommen)
to relieve [rɪ'li:v]	– erleichtern; ablösen
to reprove [rɪ'pru:v]	– tadeln
to retie [rɪ'taɪ]	– wieder festmachen, ~ ziehen
to retrieve [rɪ'tri:v]	– wiederfinden
reward [rɪ'wɔ:d]	– Belohnung
to rifle ['raɪfl]	– (aus-)plündern
to rip [rɪp]	– reißen hier: herausreißen
rotten ['rɒtn]	– gemein; blöd
to rouse [raʊz]	– aufschrecken
rubbish [rʌbɪʃ]	– Kram, Plunder

S

sales staff ['seɪlz stɑ:f]	– Verkaufspersonal
to salute [sə'lu:t]	– grüßen
to scoff [skɒf]	– spotten
scourge [skɜ:dʒ]	– Geißel, Plage
to scratch [skrætʃ]	– kratzen
security [sɪ'kjʊərɪtɪ]	– Sicherheit
securities [sɪ'kjʊərɪtɪz]	– Wertpapiere
to seize [si:z]	– packen, ergreifen
sequence ['si:kwəns]	– Reihenfolge
to set (a trap) [set]	– (eine Falle) stellen

share [ʃeə]	– Anteil
to shatter [ˈʃætə]	– zerschlagen, einschlagen
to shelter [ˈʃeltə]	– Zuflucht (Schutz) geben
to shuffle [ˈʃʌfl]	– schlurfen
silk [sɪlk]	– Seide
to skid [skɪd]	– rutschen, schleudern
slab [slæb]	– Platte; Fliese
sleeve [sli:v]	– Ärmel
sleuth [slu:θ]	– Detektiv
to snap [snæp]	– schnappen; bissig entgegnen
to snap [snæp]	– fotografieren
to sneak [sni:k]	– (herum-)schleichen
to sneer [snɪə]	– spotten, feixen
to sneeze [sni:z]	– niesen
to snort [snɔ:t]	– schnauben
socket [ˈsɒkɪt]	– Fassung, (Steck-)Dose
soil [sɔɪl]	– Erde, Boden; Dreck
solemn [ˈsɒləm]	– feierlich
in spite of [ɪn ˈspaɪt əv]	– trotz
to spot [spɒt]	– (auf-)finden, ausmachen
squad [skwɒd]	– (Militär-, Polizei-)Einheit, Kommando
squarish [ˈskweərɪʃ]	– eckig, quadratisch
to squeak [skwi:k]	– quieken, piepsen
to squirt [skwɜ:t]	– spritzen
starboard [ˈstɑ:bəd]	– Steuerbord
starry [ˈstɑ:rɪ]	– voller Sterne
statement [ˈsteɪtmənt]	– Aussage
to station [ˈsteiʃn]	– stationieren, bereitstellen

to steer [stɪə]	– steuern, führen
stocky ['stɒkɪ]	– stämmig
to stoop [stu:p]	– sich bücken
(department) store [stɔ:]	– Warenhaus, Kaufhaus
to straggle ['strægl]	– bummeln, zotteln
to straighten ['streɪtn] one's back	– sich aufrichten
strap [stræp]	– Gurt
stroke of genius [strəʊk]	– Geniestreich
(pearl-) studded ['stʌdɪd]	– (Perlen-)besetzt
suede [sweɪd]	– Wildleder
to suggest [sə'dʒest]	– vermuten lassen
superior [sju:'pɪərɪə]	– überlegen
suspect ['sʌs'pekt]	– Verdächtiger
to suspect [səs'pekt]	– vermuten
suspicion [səs'pɪʃn]	– Verdacht
to hold sway [sweɪ]	– herrschen
to make a clean sweep [swi:p]	– gründlich aufräumen, Ordnung machen

T

tangle ['tæŋgl]	– Gewirr, Durcheinander
theft [θeft]	– Diebstahl
to thin out [θin]	– weniger werden
thud [θʌd]	– Schlag
to tickle ['tɪkl]	– kitzeln; amüsieren
tie pin ['taɪpɪn]	– Schlipsnadel
to toss [tɒs]	– (Münze) werfen
trace [treɪs]	– Spur
traitor ['treɪtə]	– Verräter
treacherous ['tretʃərəs]	– verräterisch

to tug [tʌg] – ziehen, schleppen
tyre ['taɪə] – Reifen

U

umpteenth ['ʌmti:nθ] – wiederholt
unconscious [ʌn'kɒnʃəs] – bewusstlos
underwear ['ʌndəweə] – Unterwäsche
uneasy [ʌn'i:zɪ] – unbehaglich, unwohl
uneventful [ʌnɪ'ventfʊl] – langweilig
unfortunate [ʌn'fɔ:tʃnɪt] – unglücklich
unguarded [ʌn'gɑ:dɪd] – unbewacht
unimpressed ['ʌnɪm'prest] – unbeeindruckt
uninhabited [ʌnɪn'hæbɪtɪd] – unbewohnt
unshaven [ʌn'ʃeɪvn] – unrasiert
unsuspecting [ʌnsəs'pektɪŋ] – ahnungslos
to upset [ʌp'set] – verwirren, in Verlegenheit bringen
to urge [ɜ:dʒ] – drängen, anfeuern
urgent ['ɜ:dʒənt] – dringend

V

video camera ['vɪdɪəʊkæmərə] – Videokamera
vigil ['vɪdʒɪl] – Wache
villain ['vɪlən] – Schurke
violent ['vaɪələnt] – heftig
vivid ['vɪvɪd] – lebhaft
to volunteer [vɒlən'tɪə] – freiwillig etwas tun

W

wallet ['wɒlɪt] – Brieftasche
ward [wɔ:d] – Abteilung
wig [wɪg] – Perücke
wine [waɪn] – Wein

within [wɪ'ðɪn] – innerhalb
wizened ['wɪznd] – verhutzelt, schrumpelig
wrinkled ['rɪnkld] – runzelig, faltig

Y

yarn [jaːn] – Seemannsgarn